Berlin Wall 1970

Siena. Italy 1996

Marseille 1999

Monastery at Singhik, Tibetan border. 1974

For Colin McNaughton –
and dreamers everywhere

Copyright © 2002 by Michael Foreman
The rights of Michael Foreman to be identified as the author and illustrator of this work
have been asserted by him in accordance with the Copyright, Designs and Patents Act, 1988.
First published in Great Britain in 2002 by Andersen Press Ltd.,20 Vauxhall Bridge Road, London SW1V 2SA.
Published in Australia by Random House Australia Pty., 20 Alfred Street, Milsons Point, Sydney, NSW 2061.
All rights reserved. Colour separated in Switzerland by Photolitho AG, Zürich.
Printed and bound in Italy by Grafiche AZ, Verona.

10   9   8   7   6   5   4   3   2   1

British Library Cataloguing in Publication Data available.

ISBN 1 84270 085 5

This book has been printed on acid-free paper

Michael Foreman

WONDER GOAL!

Andersen Press
London

It was a cold Sunday in winter, and the boy hadn't noticed the lads tie his bootlaces together on the way to the game.
So when he tripped and fell out of the builder's van that was their team bus it just made him even more determined to 'show them'.

They were good lads really, but he was new to the team and they always teased the new boy.

And when they ran out to start
the game, he knew they all
dreamed the same dream,
the same impossible dream
of one day becoming
famous footballers.

In the second half, he got his
chance to 'show them'.

It was perfect.
Head over the ball,
balance, power, timing.
All the things his dad
had told him.

As soon as he kicked it,
he knew it was going
to be a goal.
It was a screamer.
No keeper in the world
would save that shot.

Maybe *now* his team mates
would stop teasing him.

Then in his mind,
everything seemed to stop,
frozen in time.

The keeper seemed
to hang in the air,
and the ball hovered
just beyond his fingertips.

It was like a photograph . . .

. . . like all those photographs
that crowded the walls
of his tiny bedroom,
where he dreamed every night
of scoring a wonder goal and
winning the World Cup.

He knew his dad used
to have the same dream
when he was a boy,
and that he too had slept
in a room wall to wall
with heroes.

His dad usually came
to all the games but this
weekend he had to
work overtime.
His dad was not going to
see the wonder goal.
It wouldn't be in the papers
and it wouldn't be on the telly.
And his dad was going to miss it.

All this flashed through
his mind as the ball flew
towards the goal.
And then time clicked
into gear once more
and moved on . . .

and on . . .

The keeper hit the ground . . .

. . . and the ball smacked
into the back of the net.

The vast crowd erupted.
He had hit another
wonder goal!

Just like the goal
he had scored all those
years before on that
freezing boyhood Sunday.

Maybe now, after such a goal, his team mates would stop teasing him.
They were good lads really, but he was the newest member of the squad and they always teased the new boy.

And anyway, he knew they had always shared the same dream of winning the World Cup . . .

They hadn't won it yet,
but he *had* just scored
the first goal of the Final . . .
And this time it would
be in all the papers,
and on the telly.

And this time – *this* time,
his dad was there
to see it.

Soccer in the Straits of Malacca

Football in the City of the Dead, Cairo